A Note to Parents and Caregivers:

Read-it! Readers are for children who are just starting on the amazing road to reading. These beautiful books support both the acquisition of reading skills and the love of books.

The RED LEVEL presents familiar topics using common words and repeating sentence patterns.

The BLUE LEVEL presents new ideas using a larger vocabulary and varied sentence structure.

The YELLOW LEVEL presents more challenging ideas, a broad vocabulary, and wide variety in sentence structure.

The GREEN LEVEL presents more complex ideas, an extended vocabulary range, and expanded language structures.

When sharing a book with your child, read in short stretches, pausing often to talk about the pictures. Have your child turn the pages and point to the pictures and familiar words. And be sure to reread favorite stories or parts of stories.

There is no right or wrong way to share books with children. Find time to read with your child, and pass on the legacy of literacy.

Adria F. Klein, Ph.D.
Professor Emeritus
California State University
San Bernardino, California

Managing Editor: Bob Temple
Creative Director: Terri Foley
Editor: Brenda Haugen
Editorial Adviser: Andrea Cascardi
Copy Editor: Laurie Kahn
Designer: Melissa Voda
Page production: The Design Lab
The illustrations in this book were prepared digitally.

Picture Window Books
5115 Excelsior Boulevard
Suite 232
Minneapolis, MN 55416
1-877-845-8392
www.picturewindowbooks.com

Printed in the United States of America.

Library of Congress Cataloging-in-Publication Data
Blair, Eric.
The country mouse and the city mouse : a retelling of Aesop's fable / by Eric Blair ;
illustrated by Dianne Silverman.
p. cm. — (Read-it! readers)
Summary: When the town mouse and the city mouse visit each other, they discover they
prefer very different ways of life.
ISBN 1-4048-0318-1 (Reinforced Library Binding)
[1. Fables. 2. Folklore.] I. Aesop. II. Silverman, Dianne, ill. III.
Title. IV. Series.
PZ8.2.B595 Co 2004
398.2—dc22

2003016674

PICTURE WINDOW BOOKS

The Country Mouse and the City Mouse

A Retelling of Aesop's Fable
By Eric Blair

Illustrated by Dianne Silverman

Content Adviser:
Kathy Baxter, M.A.
Former Coordinator of Children's Services
Anoka County (Minnesota) Library

Reading Advisers:
Adria F. Klein, Ph.D.
Professor Emeritus, California State University
San Bernardino, California

Susan Kesselring, M.A.
Literacy Educator
Rosemount-Apple Valley-Eagan (Minnesota) School District

Picture Window Books
Minneapolis, Minnesota

What Is a Fable?

A fable is a story that teaches a lesson. In some fables, animals may talk and act the way people do. A Greek slave named Aesop created some of the world's favorite fables. Aesop's fables have been enjoyed by readers for more than 2,000 years.

The country mouse and the city mouse
had been friends for many years.

One day, the country mouse invited
the city mouse to dinner.

The country mouse opened his heart
and his pantry.

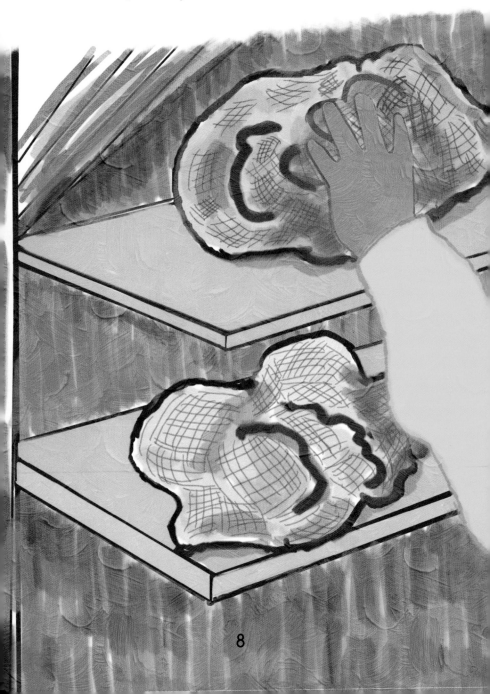

He prepared a dinner of plain country food to please his guest.

The city mouse just nibbled at the corn, barley, and peas.

He didn't like the simple dinner. He was used to eating fancier things. He talked about how good life was in the city.

"My dear friend," the city mouse said,
"aren't you bored here in the country?
We have everything in the city.

Why don't you come home with me
and enjoy the good life?"

The country mouse quickly agreed.

The two friends set off for the city.

They arrived at the city mouse's big house.
He offered a feast of beans, cheese, fruit,
and figs.

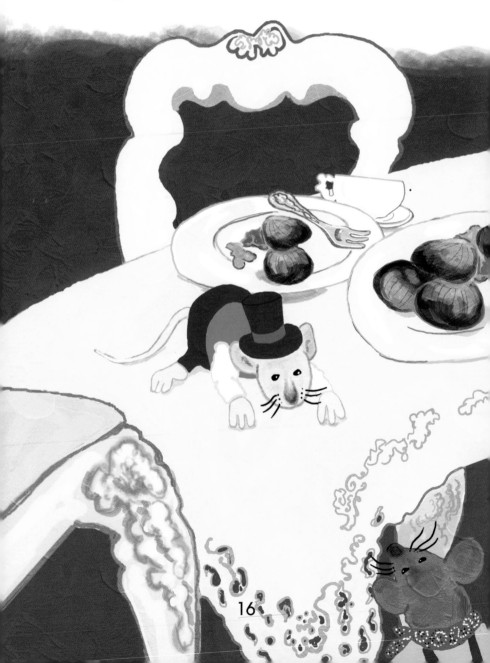

The country mouse was amazed.
He also was ashamed to be so poor.

The two friends were about to eat
when they heard a cat meow and scratch
at the door.

"Run!" cried the frightened city mouse.
The mice ran to hide in a crack.

A long time later, the two friends crept back to the table.

Just as the mice began eating some figs, servants came to clear the plates. The mice dashed to hide in dark holes.

When it was quiet, the mice came out.

"Thank you and good-bye," said
the country mouse. "I'm going home.
I'd rather live a simple life in peace
than a rich life in fear."

Levels for *Read-it!* Readers

Read-it! Readers help children practice early reading skills
with brightly illustrated stories.

Red Level: Familiar topics with frequently used words and
repeating patterns.

Blue Level: New ideas with a larger vocabulary and a variety
of language structures.

The Donkey in the Lion's Skin, by Eric Blair 1-4048-0320-3

The Goose that Laid the Golden Egg, by Mark White 1-4048-0219-3

Yellow Level: Challenging ideas with an expanded vocabulary
and a wide variety of sentences.

The Ant and the Grasshopper, by Mark White 1-4048-0217-7

The Boy Who Cried Wolf, by Eric Blair 1-4048-0319-X

The Country Mouse and the City Mouse, by Eric Blair 1-4048-0318-1

The Crow and the Pitcher, by Eric Blair 1-4048-0322-X

The Dog and the Wolf, by Eric Blair 1-4048-0323-8

The Fox and the Grapes, by Mark White 1-4048-0218-5

The Tortoise and the Hare, by Mark White 1-4048-0215-0

The Wolf in Sheep's Clothing, by Mark White 1-4048-0220-7

Green Level: More complex ideas with an extended vocabulary
range and expanded language structures.

Belling the Cat, by Eric Blair 1-4048-0321-1

The Lion and the Mouse, by Mark White 1-4048-0216-9